Dear God Kids

OUR Family

by Annie Fitzgerald

A LITTLE SIMON BOOK
PUBLISHED BY SIMON & SCHUSTER, INC., NEW YORK

Dear God,

I watched my mom today,
she really loves to cook.
I thought that she invented it,
but she gets it from a book!

Dear God,

Do you make bicycles?
They're such a lot of fun.
And if you do, would you come here
To try and make me one?

Dear God,

I have a secret place,
where I go with my Teddy,
but you don't need to find out where,
I'm sure you know already.

Dear God,

THEY SAY I LOOK LIKE DAD,
BUT I THINK THAT IS WEIRD
BECAUSE I AM A LITTLE GIRL
AND HE HAS GOT A BEARD.

Dear God,

You fix all kinds of things.
Does that include TVs?
Ours broke down just yesterday—
could you fix it, please?

Dear God,

I wish that I was tall,
as tall as my big brother.
But when I grow an inch or two,
he always grows another.

Dear God,

WHEN I'M TUCKED IN AT NIGHT,
SO SNUGLY IN MY BED,
I KNOW THAT YOU'VE BEEN LISTENING TO
THE LITTLE PRAYERS I'VE SAID.

Dear God,

I need your help today,
because I'm very late.
Would you just look and let me know
if my ribbon's straight?

Dear God,

although I'm only very small
it's lucky that I know
that if I eat my breakfast
my mother says I'll grow.

Dear God,

DO YOU HAVE BROTHERS, TOO ?
I HOPE YOU DO, LIKE ME.
THEN YOU MUST KNOW ALL ABOUT
THE FUN THAT THEY CAN BE.

Dear God,

I'M ON MY VACATION
WITH SUN AND SEA AND SAND.
I'D LIKE TO GO OUT WADING,
SO WILL YOU HOLD MY HAND?

Dear God,

THOSE ARE MY FAVORITE CUPCAKES,
I'D LIKE TO HELP MYSELF;
BUT IF I TRY TO GET TO THEM
MOM PUTS THEM ON THE SHELF.

Dear God,

This flower so small and blue
Has such a lovely bloom,
I'd like to think you made it match
The curtains in my room.

Dear God,

If I'm a Naughty Boy,
I Know you always see.
But if my Daddy Doesn't,
would you tell on me?

Dear God,

I wonder if you're tired
with all the things you do?
If you would only show me how,
could I make something too?

Dear God,

If ONLY I was TaLL,
I'D GET To see MUCH MoRe,
BUT BeING SMaLL, I Haue To Guess
WHO'S KNOCKING aT THe DOOR.

Dear God,

I'D LIKE TO THANK YOU
FOR GIVING ME THIS DAY.
IT'S FULL OF PEACE AND QUIET BECAUSE
MY BROTHER IS AWAY.

Dear God,

TONIGHT WE PUT OUR PRESENTS
AROUND THE CHRISTMAS TREE.
TOMORROW IS **YOUR** BIRTHDAY, BUT
IT'S A SPECIAL DAY FOR ME !

Dear God,

Thank you for the seasons,
the wind, the rain, and sun.
If we didn't have a winter
spring wouldn't be such fun.